THE BLUES OF FLATS BROWN

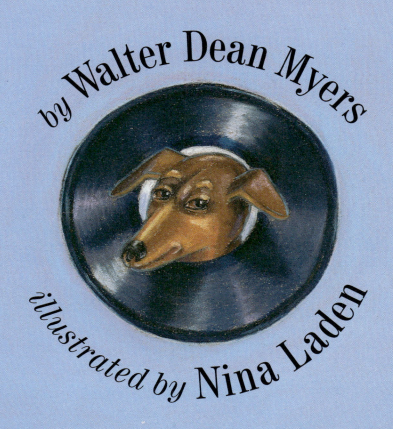

by Walter Dean Myers

illustrated by Nina Laden

HOLIDAY HOUSE / NEW YORK

To Lewis Gatewood, blues guitarist and friend extraordinaire
Special thanks to Walter and Regina for letting me play with this blues dawg
N. L.

Text copyright © 2000 by Walter Dean Myers
Illustrations copyright © 2000 by Nina Laden

All Rights Reserved

Printed in the United States of America

First Edition

The illustrations were created with pastels
on Strathmore Artagain recycled paper, in Gotham Gray.

The text typeface is Century 725 Condensed.

Library of Congress Cataloging-in-Publication Data
Myers, Walter Dean, 1937–
The blues of Flats Brown / by Walter Dean Myers; illustrated by Nina Laden.–1st ed.
p.   cm.
   Summary: To escape an abusive master, a junkyard dog named Flats runs away and
makes a name for himself from Mississippi to New York City playing blues on his guitar.
   ISBN 0-8234-1480-9
   [1. Dogs Fiction. 2. Blues (Music) Fiction.]
I. Laden, Nina, ill. II. Title.
PZ7.M992Bn   2000
[E]—dc21   99-16695
CIP

This here's the story of Flats Brown,

the blues playingest dog you ever heard of. If you ain't never heard of Flats, that's okay, because he probably never heard of you, neither.

Flats was born in a junkyard way down in Mound Bayou, Mississippi. The junkyard was owned by a man named A. J. Grubbs.

Now A. J. Grubbs was the meanest man in Mound Bayou. He was so mean he didn't even like himself. He had a little piece of mirror on the door of the hut he slept in and every time he saw his face in it, he spit on it.

Grubbs had two dogs, Flats and Caleb, and he was mean to both of them. Flats was young, no more than a teenager in dog years. Caleb was old and had a touch of arthritis in his hip, but he had a good heart.

What Flats liked to do most was play the blues. He had an old National guitar and he could just about make that thing sing! He would spend all his free time sitting and picking out tunes on that guitar and singing. Did I tell you he could sing? Man, he could sing up a storm. You hear me?

A. J. Grubbs had other ideas. He wanted Flats and Caleb to be fighting dogs so he could brag on them. One night Grubbs brought some strangers into the junkyard. They had a big, ugly bulldog with them.

"Caleb, what they fixing to do?" Flats asked.

"I think they're going to make me fight that dog," Caleb said.

"Caleb, you're too old," Flats said. "That dog will..."

"I know," Caleb said. "I know."

It was a terrible fight, with barking and growling and yelping all over the place. Caleb was hurt real bad.

"You stupid dog!" A. J. Grubbs kicked Caleb. "You're making me look stupid. Flats will fight tomorrow, and he'd better win!"

"Caleb, I'm not a fighting dog," Flats said when A. J. Grubbs had left them. "I'm a blues playing dog."

"I know," Caleb said. "We got to run away from here." That night, when the moon was behind a cloud, the two friends crawled under the fence.

"Caleb, why is A. J. so mean?" Flats asked when they had gone outside.

"Sometimes I think he's like the junk in that yard," Caleb said. "Just a throwed away man."

Flats and Caleb made their way down to Shanty Town. They lived where they could and made enough money to eat by Flats playing on the street. People would listen to him playing the blues and would throw them coins.

"Hey, you the blues playing dog everybody talking about?" a man with a gold tooth asked one day.

"Yeah, that's me," Flats said.

"Well, why don't you come play in my club?" the man asked.

That's how Flats got to play in a black club called The Curley-Que.

Every night Flats played and Caleb backed him up on the bones.
Flats put down some mean sounds. He played "The Bent Tail Blues,"
"The Mangy Muzzle Stomp," and his favorite, "The Freaky Flea Blues,"
just like he owned them. But one day, right in the middle of "The Bad
Barking Blues," who come in the door but A. J. Grubbs.

"You're my dog!" Grubbs called out. "And I'm here to get you and take
you back to the junkyard!"

Grubbs tried to drag Flats out of the club. He would have done it,
too, if Caleb hadn't chomped down on his leg. While Grubbs hopped
around on one foot, Flats and Caleb hot pawed it out the front door.
They were really scared as they took to the road again.

They didn't stop this time until they got clear to Memphis, Tennessee.

"If we keep playing on the street, A. J. Grubbs will find us again," Flats said. "I can't stand no fighting."

"Maybe you can make a record," Caleb said, looking up at a sign for Imperial Records.

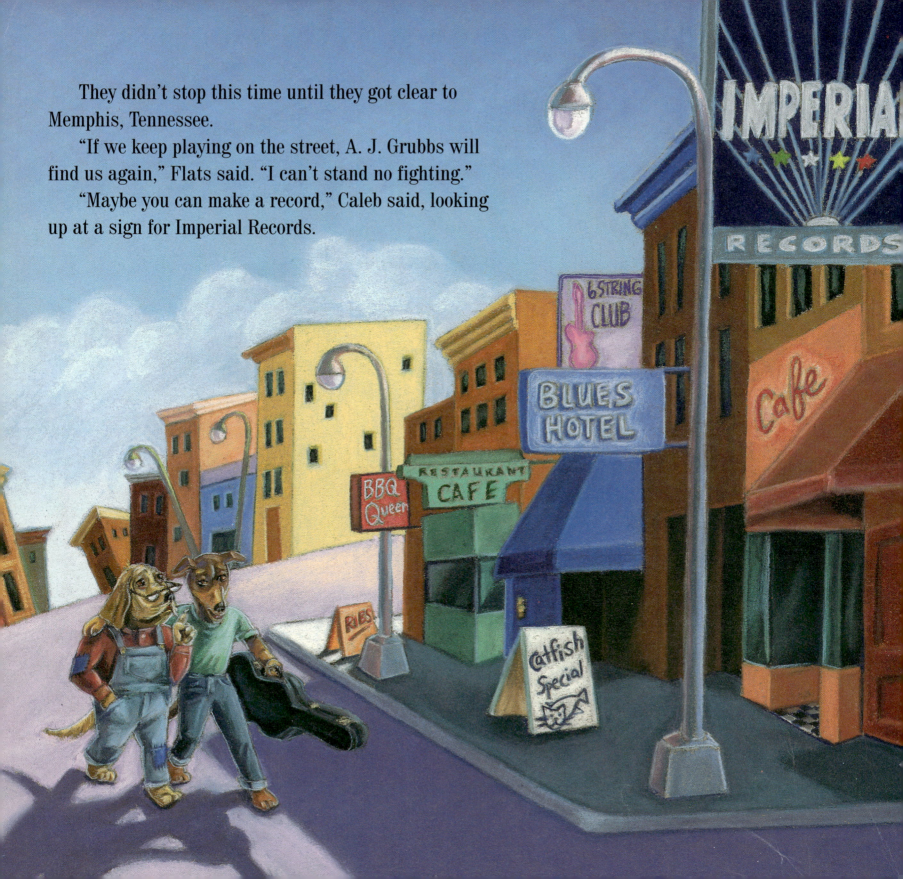

They found a little recording studio on Beale Street. The man in the studio said he never heard of a blues playing dog, but he gave Flats a chance. Flats sat on a stool and played a little song he had written himself called "The Junkyard Heap." The man hired him on the spot.

People who heard Flats's record wondered where he had come from. Some were saying he had six fingers on each paw, and some said that his wife had run off to Mexico and left him with a broken heart. None of that was true, but it sold a lot of records.

You can imagine what happened next. Old A. J. Grubbs, bad breath and all, showed up at the recording studio sweating and acting ugly.

"That dog is mine!" Grubbs hollered. "And I come to get him!"

Flats jumped out the window and Caleb ran out the back door. They ran down an alley, cut through a tent revival meeting, and didn't stop until they reached the railroad tracks. They were dead tired as they waited for a train going north. When it came, Caleb put his arms around Flats and said good-bye.

"Good-bye?" Flats looked at his best friend.

"Flats, I'm too old to be running like this," Caleb said. "You're young and you got a lot of life and a lot of music in you."

"But Caleb, we're a team," Flats said, choking back the tears.

"It's you that Grubbs is after," Caleb said. "You got to go and Caleb got to stay behind. Go on now, boy. Here comes the Midnight Special."

Flats felt bad, but he knew Caleb was right. The old dog was too beat down and too weary to run anymore.

On the train, Flats wrote a real sad song called "The Dog Gone Long Gone Blues." He dedicated that song to his friend Caleb.

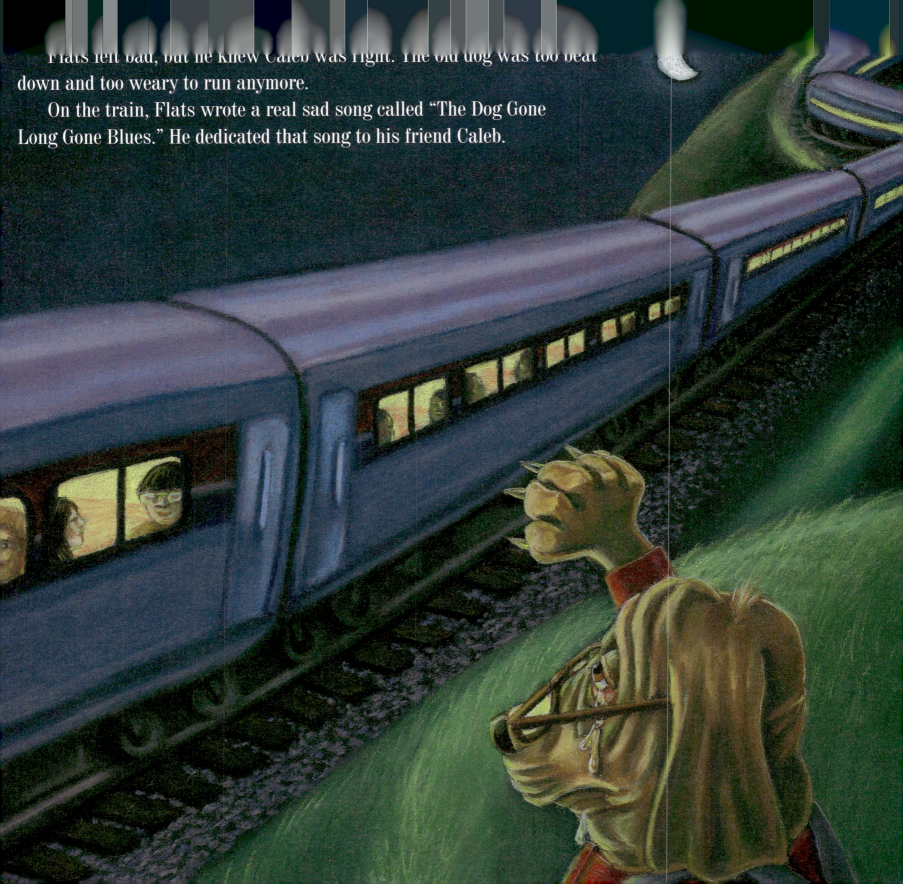

New York City was the biggest place Flats ever did see. For a while, he just wandered the streets, looking at the tall buildings and feeling as out of place as a three-legged skunk at a Georgia hoedown. By the time he found a place where they played the blues he was skinny as a rail. Blind Buddy Doyle, the king of the country blues, was the owner, and he told Flats to sit down and play.

Flats was nervous, but he started to play. He played the sounds of the waterfront in Mound Bayou and the music from the little church down the street from the junkyard. He played the lonely sounds of a freight train and the hot sounds of The Curley-Que. He really put his heart and soul in his playing.

"I might be blind," Blind Buddy Doyle said, "but I can see the dream you're playing."

Flats got the job and did good, real good. Everybody got to loving him, but I guess you know what the wind blew in one stormy night. That's right, it was A. J. Grubbs.

Soon as Flats saw Grubbs, he remembered what Caleb had said when he stayed back in Memphis. He sat down and started playing a little tune he called "The Ain't No Use Running Blues."

"I got you now!" Grubbs said. "You going back with me!"

Flats felt lower than a bowlegged worm. But then he thought about what Caleb had said, that Grubbs was just like the junk in his yard. He was a throwed away man. Flats felt bad about going back to Mound Bayou, but he felt bad for Grubbs, too.

"Mr. Grubbs, I just want to play one more tune before I go," Flats said. "This is a song I wrote called 'The Gritty Grubbs Blues.' It goes like this...."

Flats started playing "The Gritty Grubbs Blues," about a man nobody understood and everybody thought was bad because he lived in a junkyard. As Flats played, the tears started running down Grubbs's face. That song touched Grubbs deep inside, the way blues do sometimes.

"Flats, that is the best song I have ever heard," he said when Flats was done playing. "You go on playing that song, and I will go on back home and leave you in peace."

And with that, A. J. Grubbs picked himself up and walked right out the door. All he'd needed was for somebody to show him a little love.

NOW PLAYING
FLATS BROWN

After that everybody thought Flats was going to stay in New York and get filthy rich. What they didn't know was that Flats was a blues playing kind of dog, not a filthy rich kind of dog.

About a week later, Flats got his guitar, packed up some fried chicken in a cardboard suitcase, and left New York.

That was the last time anybody around there heard from Flats. Once in a while, people from Savannah, Georgia, would talk about two dogs that played the blues down near the waterfront. They say one dog played guitar and the other backed him up on the bones and their favorite tune was "The Freaky Flea Blues."

Some people don't believe that.

I do.

THE NEW YORK CITY BLUES

I got the New York City, far from down home blues
I got the New York City, far from down home blues
If you looking for true love, New York ain't what you choose

I was born in Mississippi, where the waters run so high
(I said) I was born in Mississippi, where the waters run so high
The eating's good, but the folks will make you cry

I been steady 'buked, and just as steady scorned
I been steady 'buked, and just as steady scorned
Been beat up and chased down, since the Tuesday I was born

A mojo woman said that one day I'd go far
(I said) A mojo woman said that one day I'd go far
But I can't drag my soul, past the strings of my guitar

All I see is strangers, Caleb where you be?
All I see is strangers, best friend where you be?
Won't somebody with a good heart, come and rescue me

I got the New York City, far from down home blues
(I said) I got the New York City, far from down home blues
Ain't in no union, but I sure done paid my dues

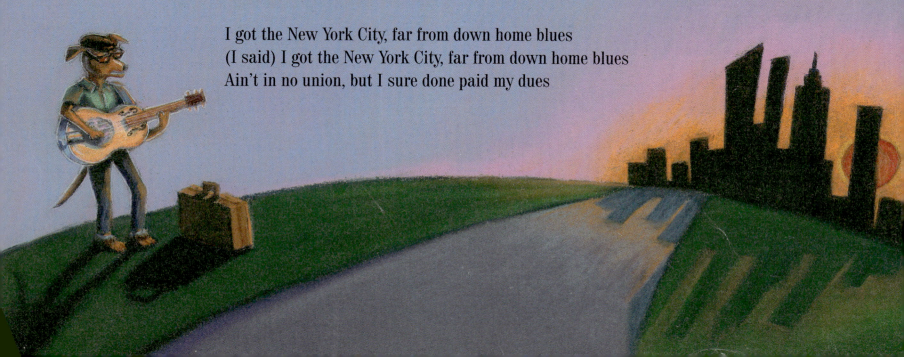